Words to Know Before You Read

dream

fairy

loose

out

pillow

tooth

under

wiggle

© 2013 Rourke Educational Media

All rights reserved. No part of this book may be reproduced or utilized in any form or by any means, electronic or mechanical including photocopying, recording, or by any information storage and retrieval system without permission in writing from the publisher.

www.rourkeeducationalmedia.com

Edited by Precious McKenzie
Illustrated by Ed Myer
Art Direction and Page Layout by Renee Brady

Library of Congress PCN Data

The Tooth Fairy / Anastasia Suen
ISBN 978-1-61810-174-7 (hard cover) (alk. paper)
ISBN 978-1-61810-307-9 (soft cover)
Library of Congress Control Number: 2012936775

Rourke Educational Media
Printed in the United States of America,
North Mankato, Minnesota

Ro urke
Educational Media

rourkeeducationalmedia.com

customerservice@rourkeeducationalmedia.com • PO Box 643328 Vero Beach, Florida 32964

The Tooth Fairy

By Anastasia Suen

Illustrated by Ed Myer

Wiggle, wiggle.

MAR 2 8 2013

Wiggle your tooth.

Wiggle, wiggle.

Wiggle it loose.

Out, out, it's out!

Under, under, under
your pillow.

Dream, dream, dream on your pillow.

Under, under, under your pillow.

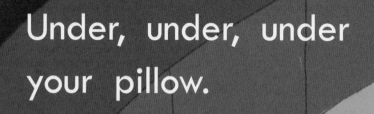

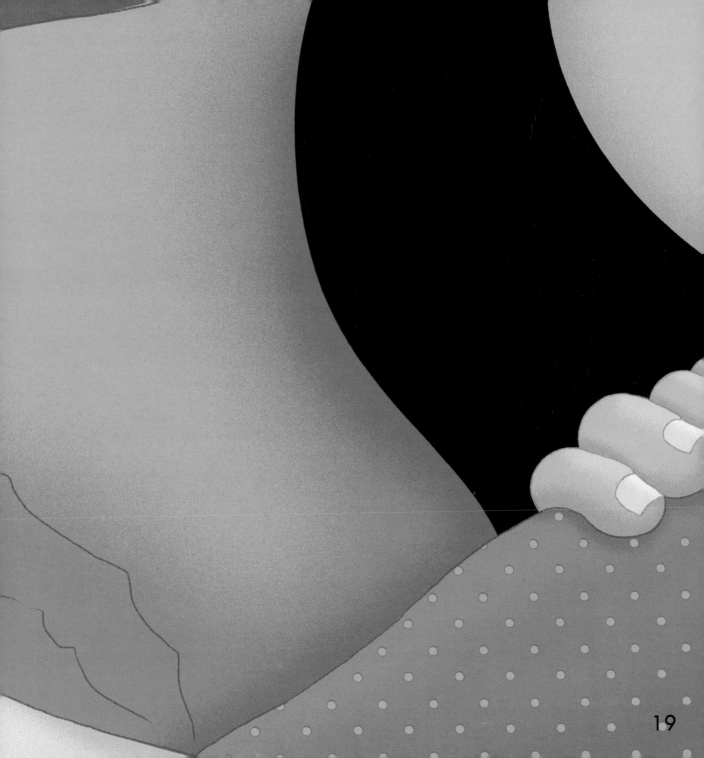

Out, out, it's mine!

After Reading Activities

You and the Story...

What was wrong with the child's tooth?
Where did the child put the tooth after it came out?
What did the fairy do in the story?
Have you ever had a loose tooth?

Words You Know Now...

In some words the same letter is written two times in a row. The word letter has **tt** in the middle. Circle the doubles you see in the words below.

dream	pillow
fairy	tooth
loose	under
out	wiggle

You Could...Check Your Mouth for Loose Teeth

- Brush your teeth to make them shiny.

- Touch each tooth.

- Do you have a loose one?

- Wiggle your loose tooth a few times.

About the Author

Anastasia Suen has taught kindergarten to college level students. She is the author of over 100 books for children and she lives with her family in Plano, Texas.

Ask The Author!
www.rem4students.com

About the Illustrator

Ed Myer is a Manchester-born illustrator now living in London. After growing up in an artistic household, Ed studied ceramics at university but always continued drawing pictures. As well as illustration, Ed likes traveling, playing computer games and walking little Ted (his Jack Russell).